Can't Seem to Make Myself Write Love Poems

Echo

Ukiyoto Publishing

All global publishing rights are held by

Ukiyoto Publishing

Published in 2025

Content Copyright © Echo

ISBN 9789370091382

*All rights reserved.
No part of this publication may be reproduced,
transmitted, or stored in a retrieval system, in any
form by any means, electronic, mechanical,
photocopying, recording or otherwise, without the
prior permission of the publisher.*

The moral rights of the authors have been asserted.

*This is a work of fiction. Names, characters, businesses,
places, events, locales, and incidents are either the
products of the author's imagination or used in a
fictitious manner. Any resemblance to actual persons,
living or dead, or actual events is purely coincidental.*

*This book is sold subject to the condition that it shall
not by way of trade or otherwise, be lent, resold, hired
out or otherwise circulated, without the publisher's
prior consent, in any form of binding or cover other
than that in which it is published.*

www.ukiyoto.com

Dedication

This poetry album is a piece of my soul, and it would not have been possible without the unwavering support of those who believed in me even when I doubted myself.

To my family—thank you for your love, patience, and encouragement. To my friends, who read my drafts and reminded me that my words matter—your support means the world.

To the quiet moments, heartbreaks, and fleeting joys that inspired these poems—you gave me stories worth writing.

And lastly, to every reader who finds a part of themselves in these pages—thank you for allowing my words to be a part of your journey.

Sincerely,
Echo

Contents

Can't Seem To Make Myself Write Love Poems   1

Nang Tahimik   3

Patutunguhan   5

Rosas   7

'di makausad   9

you were never mine to begin with   11

Guilty As Sin?   13

angst   16

I dreamt of you   18

I *loved* you so   20

maybe   23

the cut that always bleeds   26

silakbo   30

we were just poems   36

About the Author   38

Can't Seem To Make Myself Write Love Poems

Can't seem to make myself write love poems,
Not when the ink feels heavier that it should be,
Not when every word I try to weave,
Starts to unravel before it touches the page.

Can't seem to make myself write love poems,
I try—believe me, I do—
Trying to paint your name in soft pastels.
Love poems should be light,
Should dance like whispered confessions soaring high,
But mine sink, weighed down,
Flooded by doubts,
Where all I find are shadows,
Lingering where warmth should be.
Maybe, love was never really meant for my pen,

Can't Seem to Make Myself Write Love Poems

Never meant to be shaped by my hands.
I can't write love poems,
Because I never really held love—

Nang Tahimik

Tahimik akong nagmamasid, sayo'ng bawat hakbang,
Sa likod ng mga anino, naroon ang aking ngiti,
Habang sinisilayan ka, puso ko'y humihikbi.

Hindi mo alam, sa bawat saglit na ikaw nariyan,
May musika sa puso ko, ang mga salitang di kayang bigkasin,
Sa takot na baka'y lumayo ka sa akin.

Sapat na ang makita kang maligaya,
Kahit na ang sarili ko'y labis na nag-aalala.
Paano ba aaminin sa iyong mga mata,
Na ang tahimik kong mundo'y ikaw ang dahilan ng sigla.

Kung sa bawat paghinga ko'y may nais ipahiwatig,
Pakiusap, sana'y iyong madama, kahit ilang saglit.

Dahil ang tahimik kong pagmamahal ay totoo,

Hinihintay ang araw na masambit ito nang buong-buo.

Patutunguhan

Lalayo ba ako, upang makalaya?
O mananatili, kahit na nasasaktan na?
Sa gitna ng pagkalito,
Ang tanging sigurado, ikaw ang musika sa puso ko.

Ngunit, hanggang kailan ko ba titiisin?
Ang damdaming tila awit na hindi matapos-tapos awitin.
Sa bawat salita na nais kong sabihin,
Ay may namumuong takot na baka hindi mo dinggin.

Kaya't heto ako, naglalakad sa dilim,
Hinahanap ang sagot sa mga katanungang;
"ipaglalaban pa ba?"

Kung ako'y lalayo, dala ang sakit at alala,

Iiwan ko ba ang pangarap na ikaw ang kasama.

Kung mananatili sa kabila ng pagdurusa,

Hanggang kailan ba hihintayin ang tugon mo sa damdaming umaasa.

Rosas

Sa hardin ng aking puso, mas rosas na nalanta,
Sinalanta ng unos, nilunod ng pagdurusa.
Hinawakan ng mahigpit, hindi hinayaang makahinga,
Hanggang ang pag-ibig kong ito'y naging abo na.

Dumaan ang mga panahon, ngunit ang sugat ay nanatiling sariwa,
Pangakong naiwan, ngayo'y abo na.
Pinilit kong bumangon, mula sa pagkawasak ng puso,
Ngunit, paano nga ba kung hindi kita malimot?

Sinubukan kong umibig, ngunit hapdi ang naging kapalit,
Sa bawat yakap, may sugat na bumabalik.
Paano nga ba iaalay ang pusong walang laman,
Kung sa bawat paghinga, may kirot na dumaan.

Kaya't hayaan mo akong maging malaya,
Lumaya sa pagkakagapos ng pangakong wala na.
Dahil walang tunay na pag-ibig ang tutubo,
Sa pusong sinunog, sinakal ng pait at sakit ng kahapon.

'di makausad

Hindi ko na mabilang kung ilang beses
Kong sinubukan na kalimutan ka,
Binura ang mga mensahe,
Itinago ang mga alala,
Pero kahit anong gawi'y
Nar'on ka pa rin.

'Di makausad, 'di malinawan,
Ang bawat hakbang ay pilit na bumabalik sayo,
Sinusubukan kong humakbang palayo
Lumayo sa mga pangakong napako.
Ngunit kahit anong gawin ko'y,
Bakit parang yakap mo pa rin ang mundo ko.

'Di na mabura ang iyong larawan,
Tila napako, naka-ukit sa pader ng aking alaala,

Kahit pilitin ibalik ang oras,
Mga mata nating minsa'y nagmahal

'di makausad sa mga pahina ng ating istorya

you were never mine to begin with

Maybe I read too much into the way
you laughed at my jokes,
like I was the only person in the room
who ever made you feel light.

Maybe I held on too tight
To the way your voice softened
When you said my name,
As if it belonged to you
Just for a second.

Maybe I built a whole story
Out of half-written pages,
Stitched together moments
That were never meant

To be more than passing time.

Because the truth is—
You were never mine to lose.
Never mine to wait for,
Never mine to miss this much.

Guilty As Sin?

Oh, how lovely it is,
The way how the stars aligned when we speak,
How your laughter feels like a song you wrote only for me.

Every glance, every smile, every word—
Surely they mean something?
Don't they?
A spark, a sign, a story,
Waiting for the heavens to be written.

How lucky I was,
To have your gaze, our gaze lingered,
To walk beside you,
Shoulder to shoulder,
Hearts touching—

Almost.

Oh, how wonderful it was?
How the way your voice filled the silence,
How your words curled around my name like they belong to me,

How foolish, how sweet,
To believe that your eyes find mine,
To think that the warmth in your voice,
Is something more that just kindness.

Oh, what a dream it has been,
To hear you laugh at my jokes,
To memorize the way how your fingers traced the air,
As you spoke the things you love,
How we spoke about the things between us,

Was it?
How cruel it was,

Echo

To wake up from a dream,
I was never meant to have,
To realize the story I held so close
Was only ever written by me.

angst

I should have seen it-
The way your words never really held weight,
The way your touch never lingered,
Long enough to mean something.

I should have known-
When your laughter came easy,
But your heart stayed far,
When your presence felt close,
But your soul never was.

A fool-
Wasn't I?
Reading between the lines
Even when there was nothing to read,
When there was nothing written,

Searching for meaning
In a story that was never ours.

I am angry-
Not at you,
But at myself
For mistaking the way you smile
For something that never meant to be.

I dreamt of you

Does it haunts you the way it haunts me?
The echoes of laughter, in a place now silent,
The weight of a name I no longer say,
The ghost of a touch that never stayed.

I dreamt of you—
Your voice, like a song I once knew,
Your eyes, holding stories unfinished,
Your presence, as if you never left.

I tell myself I've let go,
But then the night pulls me under,
But the room still smells of our memories,
The kind that linger, uninvited,
The kind that refuse to fade.

Echo

I try to forget, I swear,
Believe me,
I do,
But forgetting is a cruel illusion.
And I wonder, for even a moment,
Do you feel it too?
Does it haunt you the way it haunts me?

I *loved* you so

I don't understand why my heart still waits,
Why it still calls for you—
Why it still aches at the sound of your name,
When you've long since stopped saying mine.

You already said I love you,
But not to me.
Not in the way I needed,
Not in the way I begged the universe for.

Still, my heart lingers,
Like a ghost haunting the ruins of a home
That never truly belonged to it,
Like a song that plays for ears
That never wanted to listen.

Echo

I tell myself I should be angry,
That I should turn this longing into rage,
But how do you hate someone
Who never promised to stay?

How do you grieve someone
Who was never yours to lose?
How do you bury a love
That still beats inside your chest?

I see you now,
Your hands holding someone else's,
Your lips spilling the words I once dreamed of,
Your love resting where I never could.

And I wonder—did you ever hesitate?
Did you ever look at me and think,
Even for a second, that maybe,
Just maybe, I was worth the risk?

Or was I just another fleeting moment,
Another name you'll forget in time,
Another lesson you never had to learn,
Because you were never the one left behind?

Still, I stay in the wreckage,
Picking up pieces of a love
That was never whole to begin with,
Pressing broken glass against my skin,
Hoping it'll make me feel something new.

And maybe one day,
I'll wake up and forget the sound of your voice,
The weight of your absence,
The way you loved—
But never me.

maybe

Maybe you liked me too,
But not enough to hold on.
Not enough to let the world know,
Not enough to fight for what could have been.

Maybe you liked me too,
Only when it was convenient,
Only when no one was watching.

I was a secret you never wanted to tell,
A fleeting thought you never dared to keep,
A fire you let burn just long enough
To warm your hands—then walked away.

You knew my heart was open,
That I would have made room for you,

That I would have been a place to stay—

You looked at me like I was almost enough,
Like I was the right person, wrong time,
Like I was something beautiful
But never yours to claim.

And for the longest time,
I convinced myself that was enough—
That being liked, even just a little,
Was better than not being seen at all.

But it wasn't enough.
Not for the way I loved you.
Not for the way I gave
And gave
And gave—only to be left empty.

And now I sit with the weight of almost,
With the ghosts of what ifs

Echo

And the echoes of words
You never had the courage to say.

I wonder if you ever look back,
If you ever let regret settle in your chest,
If you ever think of me
As more than just a passing thought.

But maybe you liked me too,
Just not enough to stay.
Not enough to try.
Not enough to make me yours.

the cut that always bleeds

I.

It started with moments, glances, unsure,

A spark too quite to call it a fire,

Yet we were, drawn like waves to the shore,

Chasing a feeling, hearts filled with desire.

II.

We were never really together– not in a way people meant,

But in between everything that wasn't said,

There was us.

A quiet unspoken truth, a fragile thing we pretended could last.

III.

Your voice was a song I played on repeat,

Your touch lingered still.

Echo

I traced our moments like lines on my skin,
But memories don't hold, no matter the will.

IV.
Then came the silence, slow and unkind,
A winter creeping into my chest.
We stood in the same rooms, breathing the past,
Yet strangers we were—no more, no less.

I tried to let go, to stitch up the wound,
But healing was cruel in a place so small.
Where your laughter still echoed, where your eyes still met mine,
And each time I saw you, I started to fall.

I built walls, I turned away,
Convinced myself I was fine.
But the heart is stubborn, the mind even more,
And your name still lingers in the back of mine.

V.

Time was meant to mend the break,
To smooth the cracks, to set me free.
But time is nothing when love remains,
And the cut that always bleeds is you and me.

VI.

I wish I could hate you, I wish I could scream,
Blame you for the ache in my chest.
But love doesn't vanish—it only transforms,
A ghost, a shadow, an unspoken regret.

VII.

So here I am, reliving the past,
Tracing the lines where you used to be.
Not together, not apart—just something in between,
A memory that refuses to leave.

VIII.

Maybe one day, I'll wake up and see,

That the wound has faded, the pain has ceased.
But until then, I'll carry this weight,
The cut that always bleeds.

silakbo

I.
They say there are five stages of grief,
To heal the heart when it starts to break.
Denial comes first, soft and slow,
Pretending you never had to go.

I set the table for two last night,
Poured your tea, left the sugar light.
I swore I heard your footsteps near,
A fleeting shadow, a whispered cheer.

Your book still rests beside the chair,
Its pages paused mid-thought, mid-air.
The world insists you've slipped away,
But I refuse to hear what they say.

Tomorrow, you'll be home again?
The door will creak, your smile will bend.
And all this silence, heavy and stark,
Will crumble like the fading dark.

II.
Then, anger, burns so bright,
"Why did you leave me alone that night?"
It shakes the world, and fills the air,
With questions shouted in despair.

"Why did you leave without goodbye?"
"Why let me fall, then teach me to fly?"
You built a home, then burned it down,
Left me drowning while you won't be found.

They say it's life, a cruel design,
A borrowed heart that was never mine.
But I can't forgive, not yet, not now—
The weight of your absence breaks my vow.

Was it too much to fight, to stay?
Couldn't love have begged you to stay awake?
I hate the stars, the earth, the sea—
For daring to exist without you and me.

III.
Bargaining follows with quiet cries,
"What if I stayed? What if I tried?"
I beg the past to change its way,
But no one listens to what I say.

If I had spoken, would you still be here?
If I had held you closer, if I had calmed your fear?
If I had called that final night,
Would it have sparked the will to fight?

I'd trade the sun, the stars, the sky,
To rewrite the moment when you said goodbye.
I'd bargain time, my breath, my name—
Anything to bring you back in my arms again.

But silence answers, cold and still,
An empty void, an iron will.
No prayer, no deal, no cosmic hand
Will return the loss I can't withstand.

IV.
Depression comes, everything heavy and gray,
Everything feels empty, and far away.
I sit in silence, lost and small,
No strength to fight, no hope at all.

The world is quiet, the clocks don't chime,
Each day a shadow, out of time.
I sit where you once made me laugh,
Now only echoes fill the gap.

I've shut the curtains, locked the door,
No visitors, no light, no more.
Your memory clings like heavy rain,
A soothing ache, a haunting pain.

V.

But then comes acceptance, soft and kind,
A place full of love inside my mind.
I see you there, in all the things I do,
A part of me that's still with 'you'.

I saw the sunrise for the first time,
Its colors bold, its rays divine.
I heard your laugh in the morning breeze,
A song of hope, a gentle tease.

I carried you here, in my heart's embrace,
Through every shadow, every space.
Though grief once ruled, its reign is done—
Your love now shines like the rising sun.

I'll tell your story, keep it near,
In whispered words and smiles sincere.
For though you've gone, your light remains—
A quiet joy through all my pain.

Echo

They say there are five stages to face,
A map through sorrow's vast embrace.
But grief is a river, wild and free,
Flowing forever, to you, from me.

we were just poems

Your laughter is a song I memorize,
A melody my heart won't dare to play.
I trace your face in the still of night,
But come morning, you're miles away.

I hold the silence between your words,
Like a fragile thread, about to break.
Your gaze, a spark I don't deserve,
Yet it's the fire I cannot forsake.

I reach, but never touch the sky,
I speak, but swallow what's within.
You're a poem I can never write,
A story I'm too scared to begin.

I write on one side of the paper,

Where my words fall, heavy yet unseen.
Each line carries a weight, a whisper,
Of a love that blooms in shadows, never green.

So I stay on this side of the paper,
Pouring love where it won't be returned.
But even if my heart is aching,
I still find beauty in being burned.

Sincerely,
Echo

About the Author

Echo

Echo is a college student with a deep passion for poetry. Through his work, he explores the complexities of love, loss, and the quiet moments often overlooked in everyday life. What began as a personal outlet for navigating his emotions and thoughts soon evolved into a powerful means of connection with others who share similar experiences.

When he's not writing, Echo enjoys playing games, listening to music, and honing his poetic craft. For him, poetry is not just a form of expression—it's a way of understanding the world and sharing his journey with every reader who turns the page.

www.ingramcontent.com/pod-product-compliance
Lightning Source LLC
LaVergne TN
LVHW041640070526
838199LV00052B/3478